"Cut & Tell"

Scissor Stories

for

Winter

by

Jean Warren

TOTLINE®
BOOKS

Warren Publishing House
Everett, WA

original
paper plate cut-outs
and
stories
by
Jean Warren

taken from back issues

of the

Totline Newsletter

ACKNOWLEDGEMENTS

Dedicated to Matthew Jay Warren, my #2 son.

ISBN 0-911019-04-9

Library of Congress Catalogue Card Number 84-051351

Cover design and story pictures by Larry Countryman, Snohomish, WA

Graphic direction and patterns by Jeff McBride, Seattle, WA

Manufactured in the United States of America.

Published by Warren Publishing House, P.O. Box 2255, Everett, WA 98203

PREFACE

For years, my family has rotated between thinking I was crazy and knowing I was crazy. For who but a disturbed person would spend all day cutting up paper plates. The fact that I enjoyed it was negated by the dishes that piled up, the beds that were left unmade and the piles of scrap plates in the living room.

But alas, there now seems to have been a reason to my madness. Stories and cut-outs to delight young children and a process to intrigue adults. Who knows, you may catch the madness and never look at a paper plate the same way again.

Seriously, the art (if I may be permitted to use this term) of paper plate cutting is fun and challenging. Many people ask how I come up with the cut-outs for my stories. Actually, I must confess, I do them backwards. First, I come up with a possible cut-out and then I write a story to fit.

Once, I was trying to come up with a paper plate crab. After a few attempts, I decided to give up on the crab because I was getting no-where. In fact, the cut-outs were beginning to resemble a frog. So I decided to try to make a frog. Twenty or more paper plates later, I finally had to admit the frog wasn't coming either — but it did vaguely resemble a spider. So why not? I'll go for a spider. Piles of plates later, when I was ready to admit that no way was I ever going to make a good spider, I looked down at my paper plate and there to my surprise was my crab!

I haven't quite figured out the creative process, but I do know you have to be free. You have to be willing to experiment and follow your instincts and be willing to go on to something new if the old doesn't work.

CONTENTS

CONTENTS

HELPFUL HINTS

STORY TELLING

Some cut-outs will stand up on their own, but others will need to be propped up to be seen. A small felt board or blackboard tray would work well.

It is also a good idea to practice cutting the cut-outs and reading the story several times before presenting the story to young children. He who hesitates and/or is unsure what to do next may lose many young listeners.

CUTTING PATTERNS

The intention of the "Cut & Tell" stories is that the story teller would mark a paper plate with cutting lines and then cut sections of the plate as they tell the story.

It is, however, not absolutely necessary to cut out the paper plate objects while reading the story. If the story teller prefers, he/she may pre-cut the plate and merely hold up the appropriate section as they reach a certain part in the story.

Pre-cut sections should be hidden from children until the appropriate time in the story to heighten the story's surprise.

HELPFUL HINTS

ADDING FEATURES

Most paper objects are fine just as they are cut out. Animal cut-outs, however, may need eyes or markings. Eyes can be made quickly with a hole punch or you can draw them on with a black marking pen.

USING THE PATTERNS

Cut-out patterns are given in two forms.

* ½ of a regular-sized paper plate with cutting lines
* A full-sized smaller circle with cutting lines, which teachers can use to make copies for themselves or their children.

The wavy edge of a real paper plate adds to the character of the cut-outs, however, plain paper is often easier to use with large groups of children. The heavier the paper used, the sturdier the cut-outs will be.

Permission is granted from Warren Publishing House for teachers to make copies of the cut-out patterns to use with students.

USING THE STORIES
WITH CHILDREN

PRESCHOOL CHILDREN

Young children love hearing the story repeated again and again as you re-cut additional paper plates. Take advantage of this repetition and begin letting the children finish parts of the story or tell what is going to happen next.

After children have heard the story many times, ask them to tell you step-by-step, what happens next in the story.

Make a cut-out for each of your children and let them paint or color the cut-out as a follow-up activity.

Preschool children would also enjoy using the non-three dimensional cut-outs as circle puzzles. Give them the cut-out pieces and let them figure out how it all goes back together into a circle shape. Cut-out stories that would make good puzzles are: The Spirit of Christmas, Mr. Snowman's Ride, The Wishing Fish and Santa's Jet Sleigh.

USING THE STORIES WITH CHILDREN

KINDERGARTEN CHILDREN

If you are working with kindergarten children you can do all of the above mentioned activities, plus more advanced ones. Kindergarten children should be able to retell the story more completely on their own. In fact, they should be able to retell the story to you as you re-cut another paper plate.

Kindergarten children should also be able to decorate their own cut-outs more elaborately. Many of them may be able to cut out their own paper plates, as the teacher re-reads the story.

FIRST AND SECOND GRADE CHILDREN

First and second grade children should be able to cut out their own cut-outs and decorate them.

They can also write or read the story on their own if the teacher would re-write it on a large story chart or run off mimeographed copies of the story for each child.

THE SINGING DREIDL

THE SINGING DREIDL

A few days before Chanukah, Sarah filled a basket **(1)** with eggs and set out for the market. She planned on trading the eggs for a present for her mother. Sarah loved going to the market and seeing all the wonderful things for sale.

Sarah wished she could buy her mother a brass candle holder, but they were much too expensive. Perhaps her mother would like a new comb or a package of needles. While Sarah was looking at all the gifts **(2)** she saw a small dreidl (Drā dle) and before she knew what had happened, she had traded all her eggs for the top.

Sarah loved the little top, but she wasn't sure it was what her mother would want. Sarah picked up the dreidl and gave it a try. It started to sing, and that is no lie! "Spin, spin, spin my top — may you be lucky when I stop."

"Oh, what a wonderful top!" cried Sarah. Everyone around her wanted to spin the magic top and listen to it sing. Everyone wanted to play the spinning game with Sarah.

Before long, Sarah had won enough money to buy something really nice for her mother. **(3)** Sarah walked down one aisle of the market, then another and another, searching for the perfect gift. At last, she found just what she was looking for, a brass menorah (candlestick holder). (The Chanukah menorah is called a Chanukiah.) **(4) (5) (6)**

Sarah was excited. This would surely be the best Chanukah ever and she was right. The sparkle in her mother's eyes when she saw her gift was matched only by the glow from the Chanukah candles in the beautiful new menorah.

CUTTING DIRECTIONS

(1) Fold the circle in half and hold it up for the basket.

(2) Cut the basket in half, then cut out the dreidl.

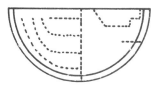 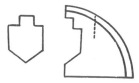

(3) Pick up the remaining half of the basket and start cutting the lines.

(4) Stand up the portion of the paper plate from which the dreidl was cut.

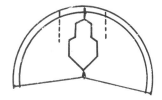

(5) Open the other half of the plate (bend sections in and out a bit to separate).

(6) Place the top of the candelabra on top of the base.

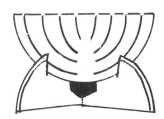

EXTENDED ACTIVITIES

Counting Game

      To celebrate Hanukkah, make a dreidl for your children. A dreidl is a four-sided top. The game you play with it is great for learning quantities and amounts.

Materials: A square cardboard box, pencil, marking pen, beans.

Preparation: Make a square top by sticking a pencil through the top and out the bottom of a small closed box. If you don't have a box, make one out of cardboard. Mark each of the four sides of the top with one of these markings: 0, All, ½, 1.

Activity: Give each child 10 beans. Each player puts a bean in the pot before every player's turn. Have each child take turns spinning the top. The children either win beans or give up beans, depending on what they spin: If the top lands on 0, the player gets nothing, if it lands on All, the player gets the whole pot; if it lands on ½, the player gets half the pot; and if it lands on 1, the player must add one to the pot.

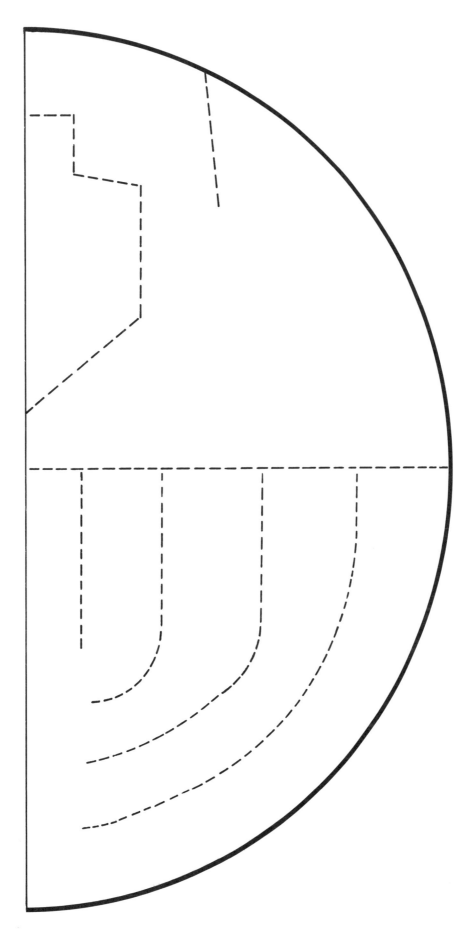

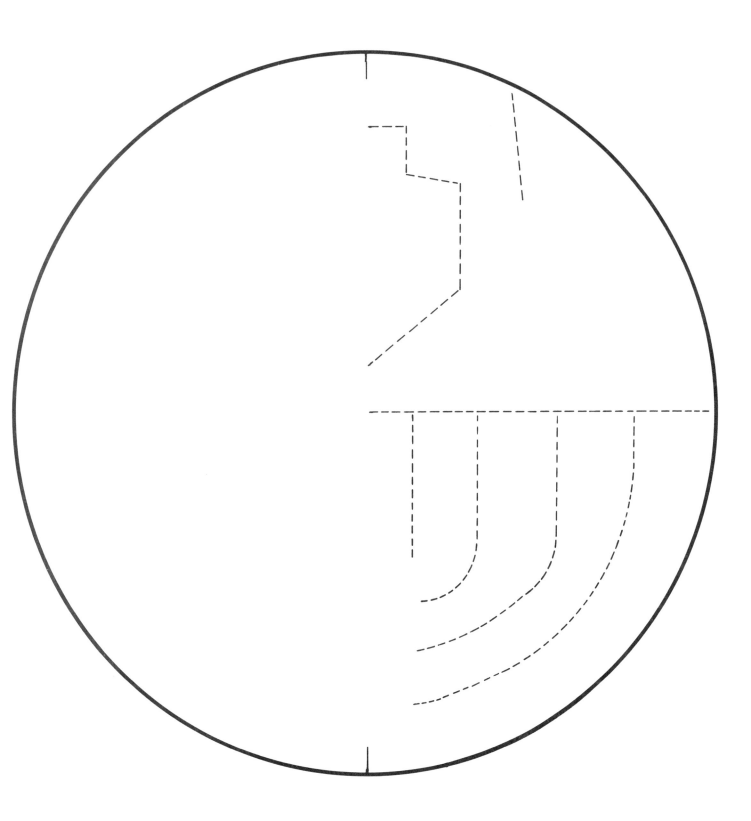

GLORIA'S CHRISTMAS ANGEL

GLORIA'S CHRISTMAS ANGEL

Once upon a time, there was a little girl named Gloria. It was near Christmas and Gloria was unhappy because she did not have a present to give her mother.

Gloria sat looking out at the stars one night wishing for a miracle. All of a sudden a beautiful angel appeared and handed Gloria a large white circle that sparkled and glowed like the moon. **(1)**

Gloria carefully folded the circle, **(2)** stuck it into her pocket and hurried downstairs to give the gift to her mother. In the excitement, however, Gloria tripped and the circle broke into many pieces. **(3)**

Gloria began to cry, for now her beautiful gift was ruined. Gloria's mother heard crying and came to see what was the matter. Gloria showed her the broken circle.

"Don't cry Gloria. It's the thought that counts," and she picked up the broken circle and started to open it. **(4)**

"Why Gloria, you were only teasing. What a beautiful surprise. This is the nicest present I have ever had." **(5)**

Gloria looked up and saw her mother holding a beautiful Christmas Angel, which her mother proudly placed on top of their Christmas tree. **(6)**

CHRISTMAS IS TRULY A TIME FOR MIRACLES!

CUTTING DIRECTIONS

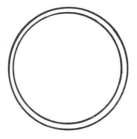

(1) Hold up full paper plate.

(2) Fold circle in half.

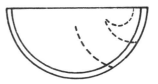

(3) Cut circle on dotted lines.

(4) Open up circle and fold down angel's arms.

(5) Fold skirt down and hook together in the back.
(Hooking directions pg. 77)

(6) Hold up completed angel.

EXTENDED ACTIVITIES

Crafts

Cut out an angel for each of your children and let them decorate it with crayons or marking pens.

Use the angels to make a large hanging mobil of angels.

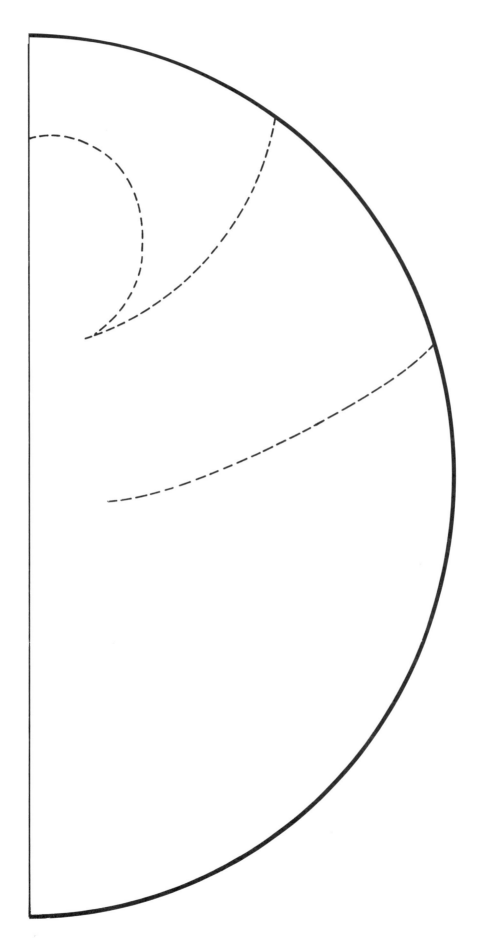

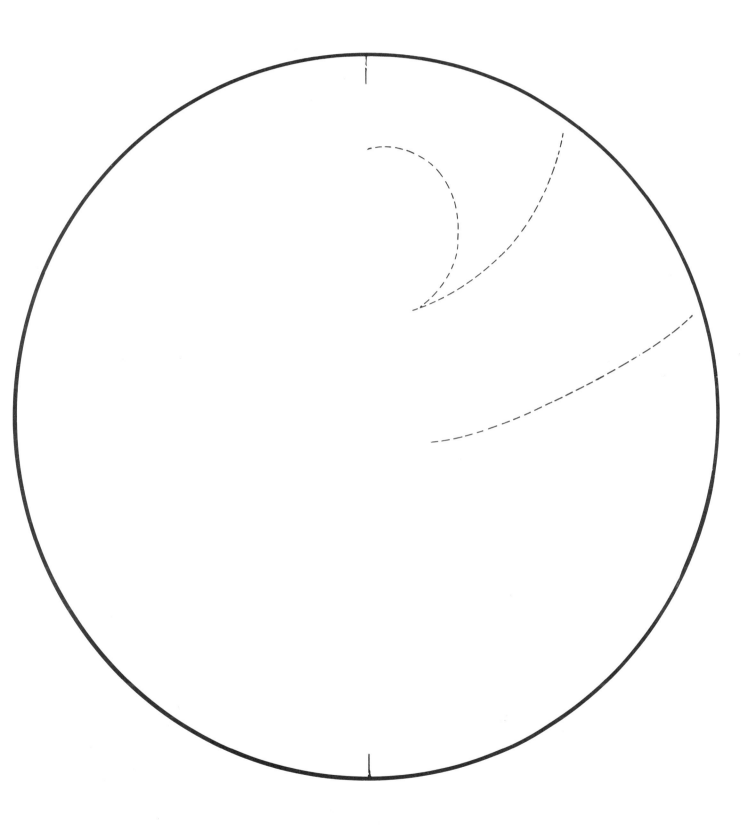

SANTA'S JET SLEIGH

Each year Santa's sleigh ride to deliver toys took longer and longer. Each year there were more and more houses to visit and more and more toys to carry. Santa grew worried. He didn't want to disappoint any good boys or girls, yet his sleigh was overcrowded and couldn't travel very fast. Something had to be done. **(1)**

One day Santa called for Rudolph, **(2)** the smartest of his reindeer. "Oh, Rudolph," said Santa, "What can I do? Christmas is coming and I'm afraid we will not be able to deliver all the toys this year."

"Don't worry Santa," said Rudolph, "I will think of something."

Rudolph went over to the toy shop and called together all of Santa's elves. Soon they had a plan. They worked and worked **(3)** and the night before Christmas, they presented Santa with **(4)**

A BRAND NEW JET SLEIGH!

"Oh!" cried Santa, "How wonderful. Now we will be able to go faster and deliver all of our presents."

Santa thanked the elves for all their hard work and gave them each a new outfit.

Then he reached into his bag and pulled out a special gift for Rudolph. **(5)**

A JET HELMET!

"Oh, thank you," said Rudolph, as he placed the helmet on over his antlers. **(6)** "Captain Rudolph reporting for take off!"

CUTTING INSTRUCTIONS

(1) Cut out Rudolph's head.

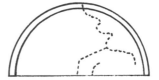

(2) Fold back antlers.

(3) Cut out sleigh and helmet.

(4) Hold up sleigh (mark with stars if you wish).

(5) Hold up helmet (mark with stars if you wish).

(6) Put helmet on Rudolph.

31

EXTENDED ACTIVITIES

Music

"Oh, He'll Be Driving A Jet Sleigh"
Sung to the tune of: "She'll Be Coming 'Round The Mountain"

Oh, he'll be driving a jet sleigh when he comes.
Oh, he'll be driving a jet sleigh when he comes.
He'll be driving a jet sleigh
He'll be driving a jet sleigh
He'll be driving a jet sleigh when he comes.

Oh, he'll be piled up with toys when he comes.
Oh, he'll be piled up with toys when he comes.
He'll be piled up with toys
For the good girls and boys.
He'll be piled up with toys when he comes.

Oh, he'll be dressed all in red when he comes.
He'll be dressed all in red when he comes.
He'll be dressed all in red,
From his toes up to his head.
He'll be dressed all in red when he comes.

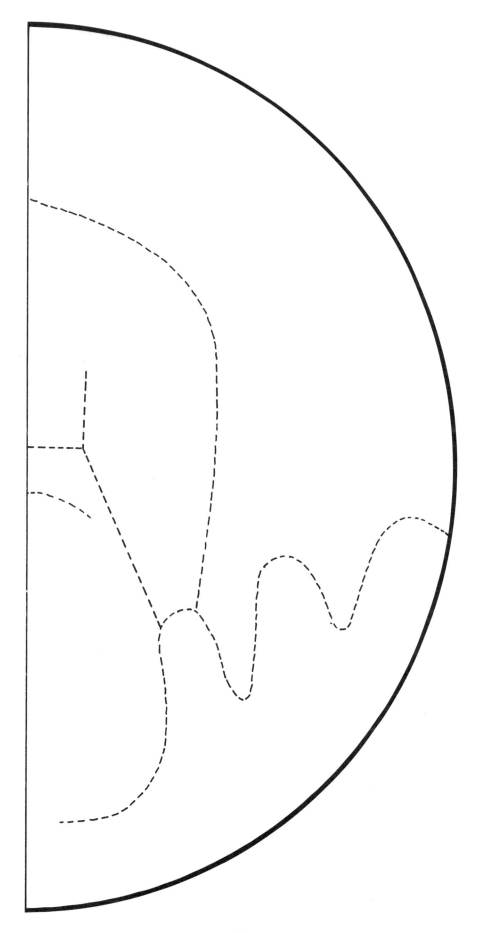

33

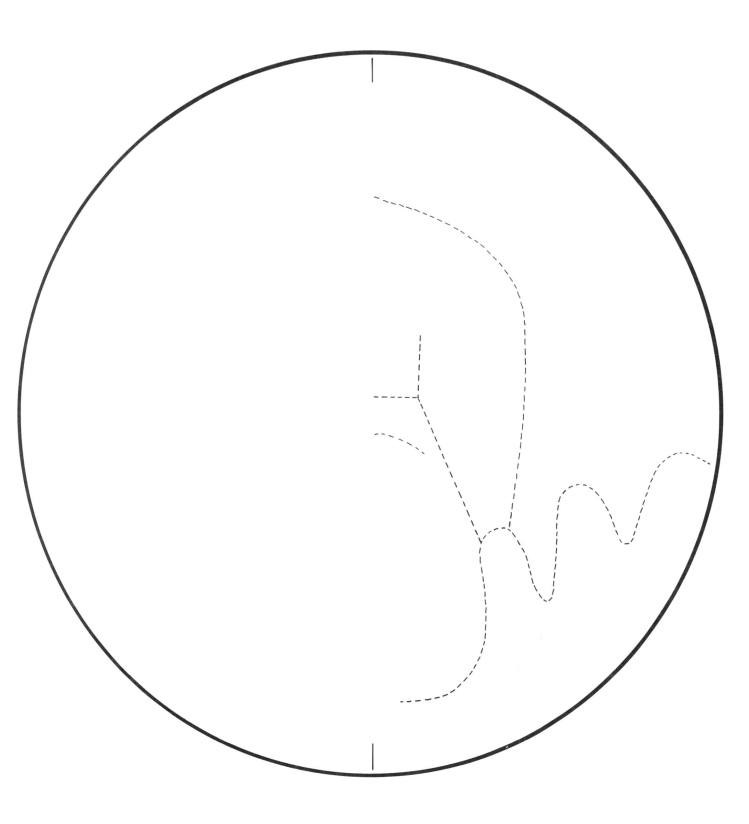

35

THE SPIRIT OF CHRISTMAS

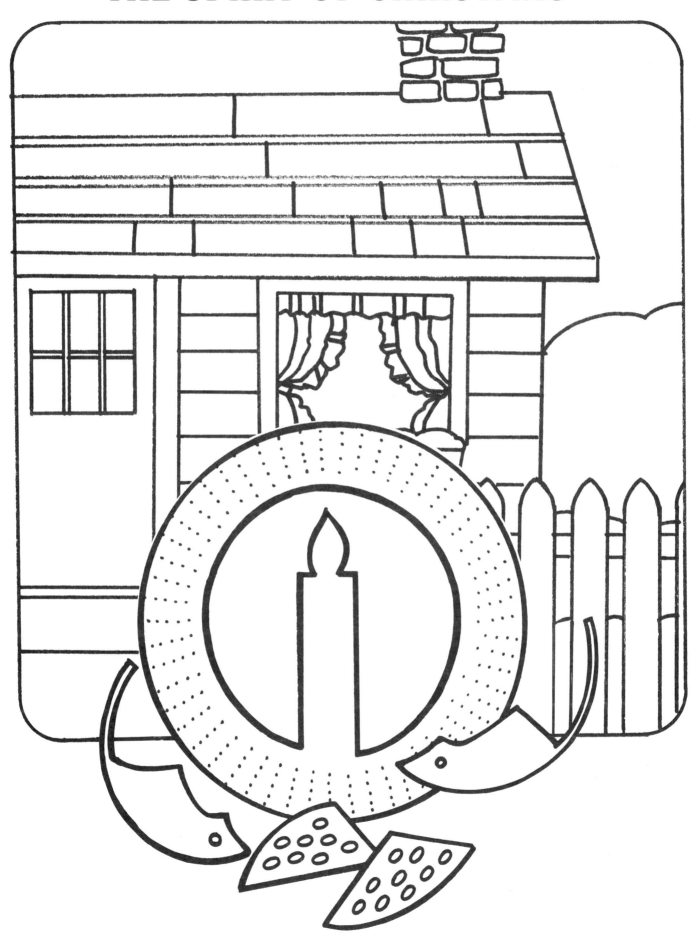

THE SPIRIT OF CHRISTMAS

(1) One Christmas Eve, long ago, there lived a little old lady in a small cottage. She lived all alone except for two mice that lived behind her stove. **(2)**

The old lady was very poor. All she had left in her cupboard were two pieces of cheese. **(3)**

Instead of eating the cheese herself, the old lady decided to give the pieces of cheese to the mice as a present. She set out the cheese and went to bed. That night when the mice came out to look for food, what a big surprise! They were so happy, what a wonderful Christmas they would have. But they also felt sorry for the old lady and sad because they had nothing to give to her in return. So they wrapped up the cheese and took it to the market where they sold it and used the money to buy a present for the old lady.

They bought a big red candle and when they got home, they decorated it with fir boughs. They hung it in her window and went to bed. **(4)**

In the morning, the old lady was ever so pleased with her surprise. Even though she was cold and hungry, the wreath made her happy. That evening she lit the candle and its glow filled her room and her heart. Its sparkle twinkled in her eyes.

Then she had another surprise and another. Friends started arriving bringing gifts. One brought her a tree, another brought some firewood, others brought food and presents. "My goodness," cried the old lady, "why have you all come?" "We saw your candle," they answered. "We knew we would find the spirit of Christmas here, so we all wanted to come." Everyone stayed and they all had a marvelous time, even the two little mice.

CUTTING INSTRUCTIONS

(1) Fold the paper plate and begin cutting as shown — as you begin the story.

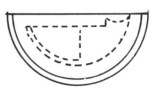

(2) Using a hole punch, punch out an eye for each mouse and hold them up for your children to see. Display mice where they can be seen.

(3) Using the hole punch, punch out holes in the pieces of cheese and hold them up for your children to see.

(4) Open up the candle and hold it up.

EXTENDED ACTIVITIES

Crafts

Cut out a wreath for each child. Let them paint or color the outside wreath green and the candle in the middle red.

Discussion

Discuss with your children the joy of giving to others.

Snack

Have a mouse snack of cheese and crackers.

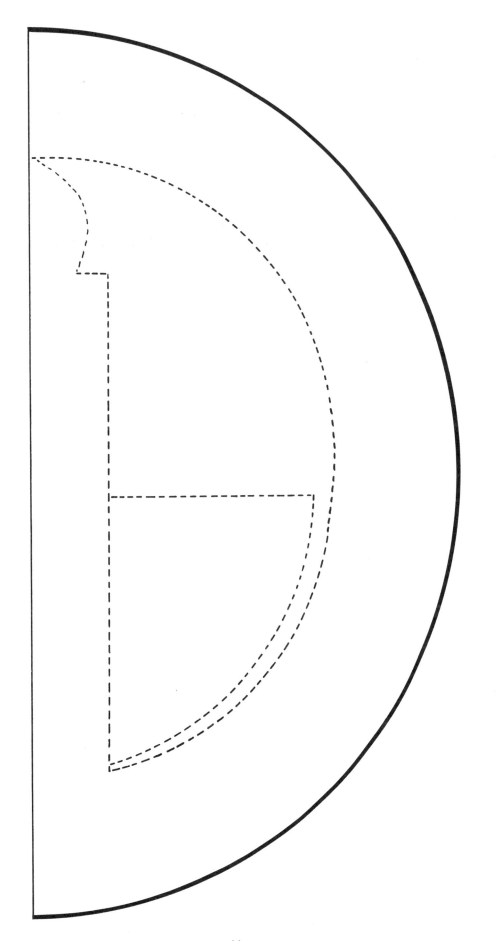

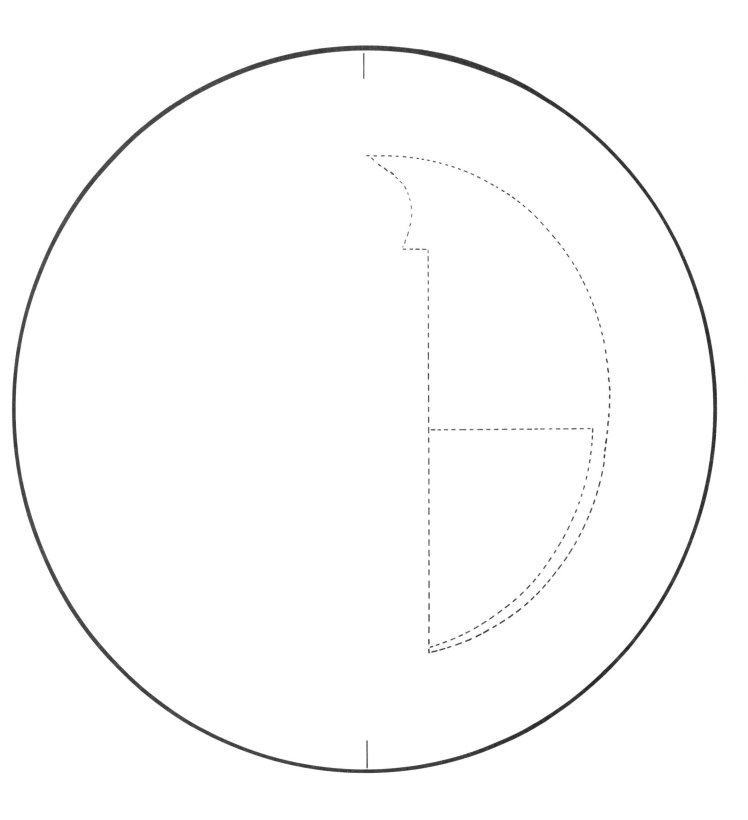

MR. SNOWMAN'S RIDE

MR. SNOWMAN'S RIDE

It had snowed at last. The children dressed warmly and hurried out to the front yard to play. First they rolled a large snowball **(1)** and then they rolled a smaller one. "Let's make a Snowman!" they cried. **(2)**

So they lifted the smaller ball on top of the big snow ball. They cut a potato in half for *eyes*, stuck a long carrot in for a nose, wrapped a long red scarf around his neck and placed a tall black hat on his head. **(3)**

The children loved their snowman and spent most of the morning dancing around him. After lunch, the children noticed that a small pond in the backyard had frozen completely over. "Let's go slide on the ice!" they all cried. So they hurried to the pond to slip and slide.

Everyone was having a good time except Mr. Snowman. Now he had no one with which to play. Tears rolled down his cheeks and froze into long icicles. Soon, the children began to miss the Snowman, too. They wished that he could watch them as they played in the backyard.

At last, they decided what they could do. They took their largest sled **(4)** into the front yard and lifted Mr. Snowman up on top. **(5)**

The children pushed and pulled and finally they managed to get Mr. Snowman into the backyard. Now everyone was happy. Watching the children made Mr. Snowman happy and playing near their snowman, made the children happy.

Soon Mr. Snowman's icicles were gone and on his face was a great big smile!

CUTTING DIRECTIONS

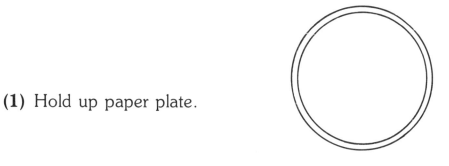

(1) Hold up paper plate.

(2) Cut on dotted lines.

(3) Open up the snowman. (decorate him if you wish)

(4) Hold up sleigh.

(5) Stick the snowman onto the sleigh.

EXTENDED ACTIVITIES

Music

THE SNOWMAN

Sung to: "The Muffin Man"

Have you seen the snowman,
*   the snowman, the snowman.*
Have you seen the snowman
*   that lives in our front yard.*
He has two brown potato eyes
*   potato eyes, potato eyes*
He has two brown potato eyes
*   and lives in our front yard.*

He has a big black top hat,
*   top hat, top hat.*
He has a big black top hat
*   and lives in our front yard.*

He has an orange carrot nose,
*   carrot nose, carrot nose.*
He has an orange carrot nose
*   and lives in our front yard.*

He has a long red woolen scarf,
*   woolen scarf, woolen scarf.*
He has a long red woolen scarf
*   and lives in our front yard.*

He has a great big smiley face,
*   smiley face, smiley face.*
He has a great big smiley face
*   and lives in our front yard.*

Crafts

Cut out a snowman for each of your children and let them decorate their snowman with marking pens.

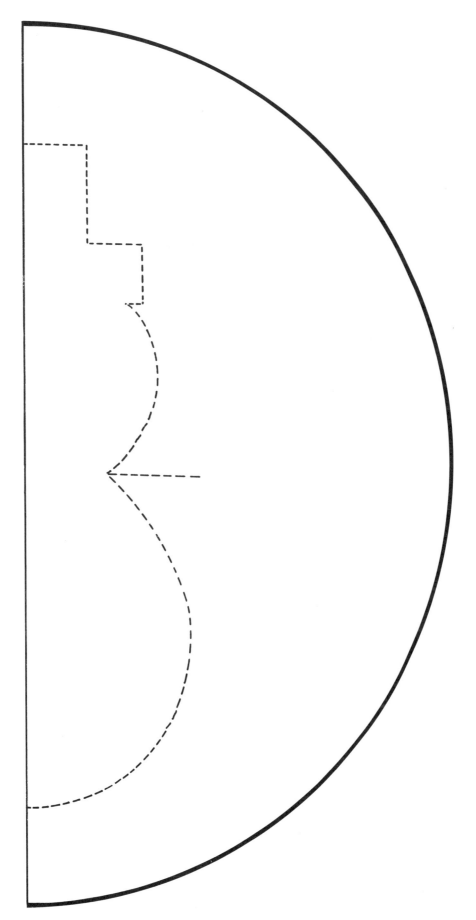

49

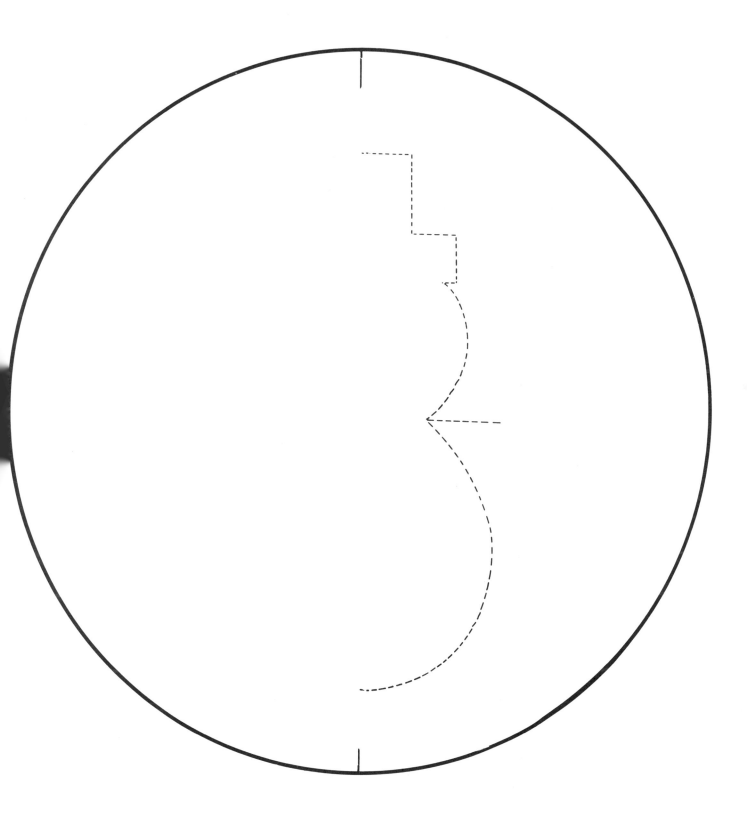

THE WISHING FISH

THE WISHING FISH

Way down South **(1)**
Lived a little palm tree **(2)**
Who sat in the sun
By the big south sea.

She loved the sun
But do you know
She wished she lived
Where it would snow.

Way up North **(3)**
Lived a little fir tree
Who stood in the snow
By the big north sea.

The fir tree loved
The cold white snow
But often wished
To the sun could go.

Now out in the sea
Lived two special fish **(4)**
Who had the power
To grant you a wish.

"I want to go North,"
cried the little palm tree
Just as one fish
Swam by in the sea. **(5)**

"I want to go South,"
The fir did sigh
As the other fish
Came swimming by. **(6)**

They both got their wish
That very same day.
They both went to lands
That were far away.

The fir tree loved
The sun in the sky
But soon his branches
Began to dry.

The palm tree loved
To watch the snow
But soon her branches
Were too cold to grow.

"Oh, dear me,"
Both trees did cry.
If we stay much longer
We will surely die.

We should have been happy
We should have been glad
With where we lived
With all we had.

The trees had a problem
And that was no lie.
Lucky for them
The fish swam back by.

"We wish, oh we wish
Never to roam
If only we could
Go back to our home."

Presto, like magic
Their wishes came true.
Both were back home
With branches all new.

Never again
Did they wish to be
Anywhere else
Than by their own sea.

CUTTING DIRECTIONS

(1) Cut out trees and corner slits.

(2) Circle back the base sides of the palm tree. Hook ends together (directions pg. 77) so tree will stand.

(3) Fold out the fir tree, hook it in the back to stand up.

(4) Draw eyes and rainbow lines on the fish if you wish. Hold up fish.

(5) Hook a fish in the slot in front of the palm tree.

(6) Hook a fish in the slot in front of the fir tree.

EXTENDED ACTIVITIES

Science

Winter is a fun time of the year to study climates. Discuss plants and animals that live in hot or cold climates.

Dramatics

On a drab winter day, take a pretend trip to a South Sea Island with your children. Make grass skirts out of newspapers and paper flower leis. Sit on a blanket in the middle of the room and shine a reading lamp down on your blanket. Have a picnic.

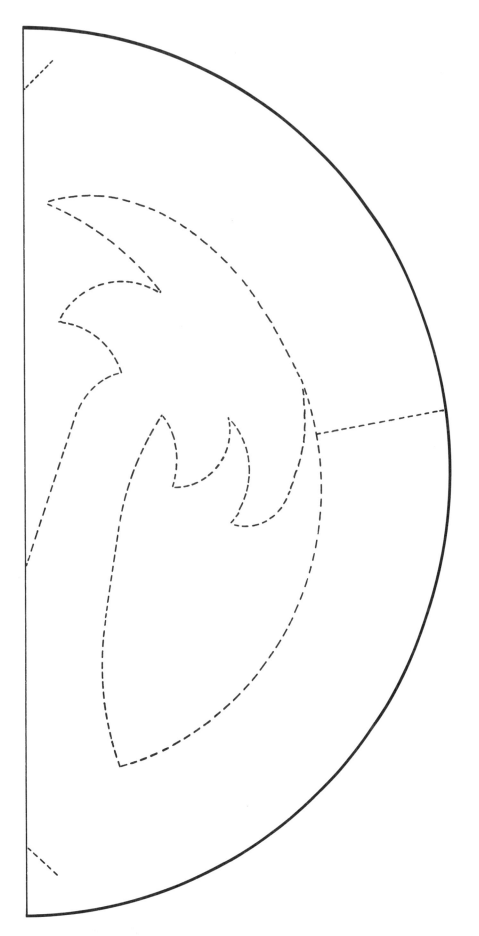

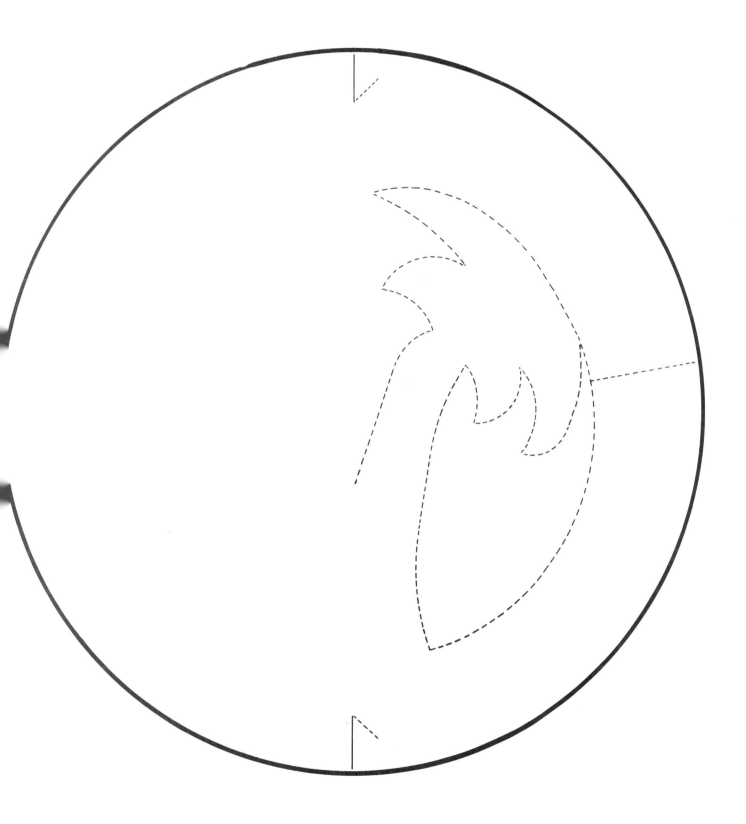

LITTLE GEORGIE GROUNDHOG

LITTLE GEORGIE GROUNDHOG

Way deep down
In a hole in the ground **(1)**
Lived little Georgie Groundhog
All furry and round. **(2)**

Little Georgie Groundhog
Popped up one day, **(3)**
He looked around
and decided to stay.

But just as Little Georgie
Started to play
Out popped his shadow **(4)**
And frightened him away. **(5)**

Back down his hole
Little Georgie sped **(6)**
Back to his home
Back to his bed!

CUTTING DIRECTIONS

(1) Fold paper plate and cut out Groundhog and shadow as shown.

(2) Fold back both Groundhog and shadow and hold up the hole.

(3) Fold up Georgie.

(4) Fold out Georgie's shadow.

(5) Fold back Georgie.

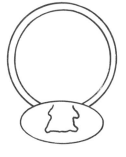

(6) Fold back everything so that only the hole shows.

63

EXTENDED ACTIVITIES

Dramatics

Legend has it that on February 2, Mr. Groundhog wakes up from his long winter's nap and goes outside. They say that if he sees his shadow, he is frightened and runs back inside his hole and sleeps for six more weeks, making the coming of spring very late.

If Mr. Groundhog does not see his shadow, he stays outside to play, indicating that spring has arrived.

Let your children take turns being Mr. Groundhog, popping up out of his hole (large cardboard box works great) while everyone recites:

> *Groundhog, groundhog popping up today*
> *Groundhog, groundhog can you play?*
>
> *If you see your shadow — run away*
> *If there is no shadow, you can stay*
>
> *Groundhog, groundhog popping up today*
> *Groundhog, groundhog can you play?*

Rig up your room so that you can create or take away a shadow. Overhead lights should eliminate the shadow and low lights aimed directly at the Groundhog should cause a shadow.

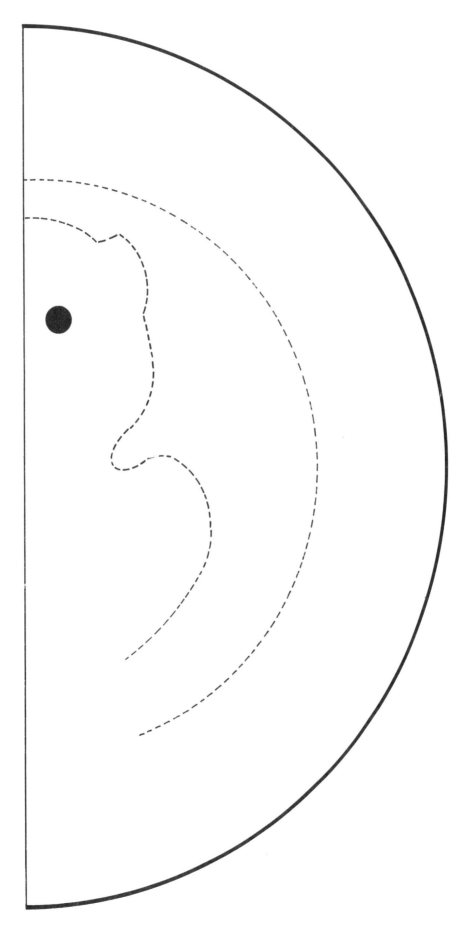

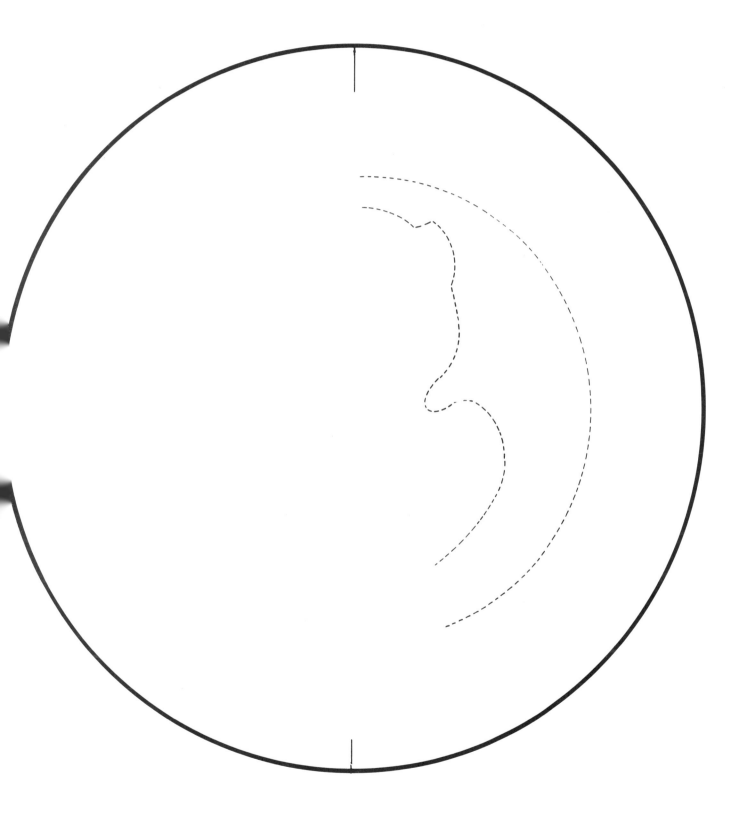

THE QUEEN OF HEARTS

THE QUEEN OF HEARTS

One day the Queen of Hearts was making tarts. She was busy rolling out her dough, **(1)** folding it over and cutting out heart shapes. **(2)**

She made two heart tarts, put them in the oven, then set them on the window ledge to cool. When she went back later to get the tarts, they were gone. "Oh no!" cried the Queen. The King will be mad if he has no tarts for dinner.

It was almost time for supper. What could the Queen do? Quickly she ran through the palace and set all the clocks back one hour. Then she hurried back to the kitchen and cut out more tarts. **(3)**

She popped more tarts into the oven, baked them, then set them in a safe place to cool. Next she went and got dressed for dinner. **(4)**

When the King sat down for dinner, out walked the Queen with his tarts. **(5)** The King was especially hungry that day and the tarts tasted extra good!

The Queen of Hearts
She made some tarts
On a Winter's day.

The Knave of Hearts
He stole those tarts
And quickly ran away.

The King of Hearts
He wanted tarts
Or it would spoil his day.

The Queen of Hearts
Could make more tarts
But a joke she'd have to play.

The Queen of Hearts
She baked more tarts
Then put them safe away.

The King of Hearts
He ate the tarts
And had a happy day.

CUTTING DIRECTIONS

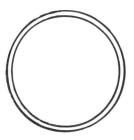

(1) Hold up circle.

(2) Fold the circle and cut out two hearts.

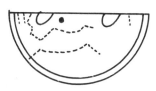

(3) Finish cutting the other lines.

(4) Fold out the Queen and her dress.

(5) Cut slits in back of dress to hook it together.

(6) Fold out the tart tray and
place the tarts on the tray.

EXTENDED ACTIVITIES

Cooking

Use heart cookie cutters to make heart cookies with your children. Or let your children make heart jelly sandwiches by cutting bread with a heart cookie cutter and then spreading the bread heart with red jam.

Dramatics

Let your children act out the story or the rhyme. Let someone be the Queen, the Knave and the King.

Party Game

Play a game similar to musical chairs. Give each child a paper heart. Have the children place their hearts on a table (or on the floor) in the middle of the room. Have the children walk around the table while you play some type of music (radio, record, etc.) While the music plays, the Knave of Hearts (you or another child) sneaks in and steals one of the hearts. When the music stops each child tries to grab a heart. The child who does not get a heart leaves the game and becomes the next Knave. The last one or two children in the game are the winners. Don't give a special prize to the winner. Winning should be enough. Be sure that everyone ends up with a paper heart at the end of the game.

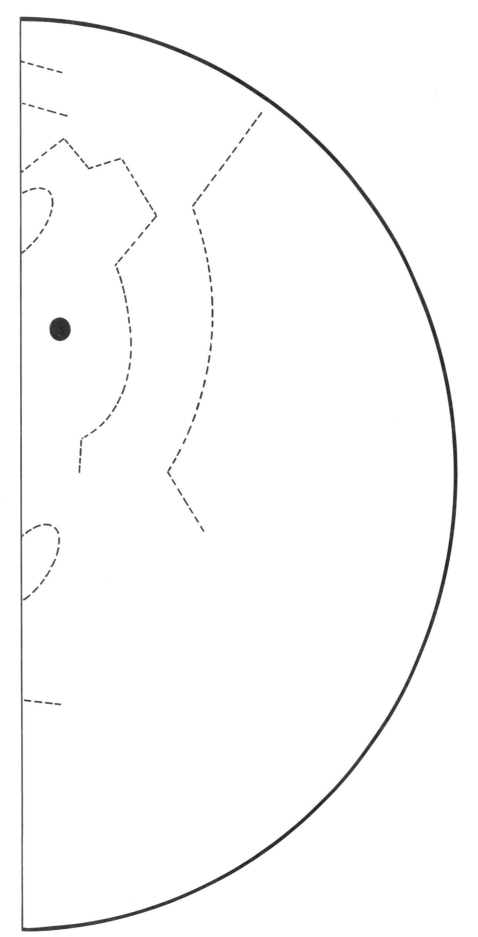

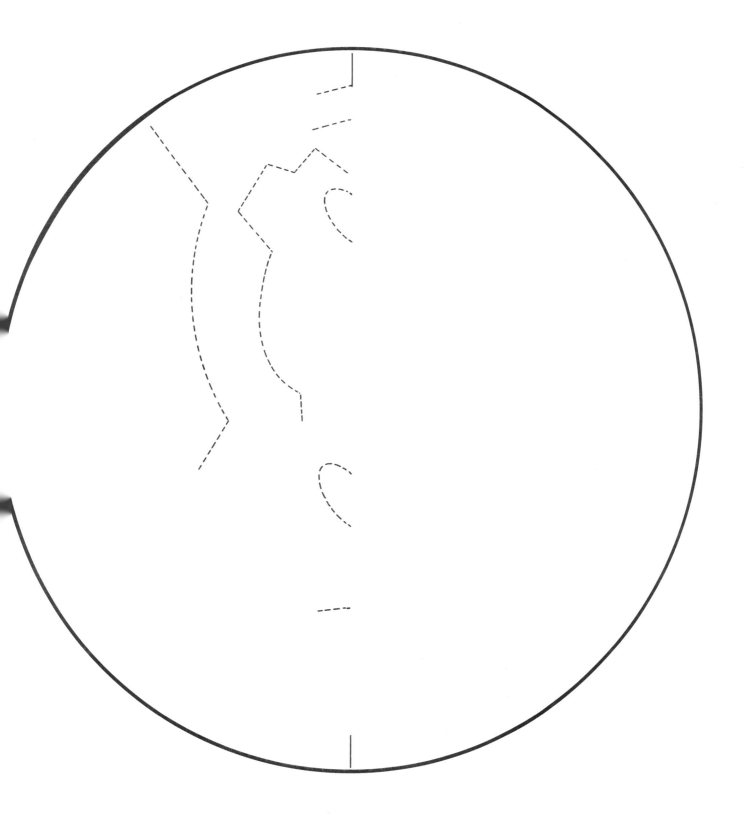

BACK HOOK-UPS

Below are directions for hooking two sides together so that a cutout can stand up on its own.

Bring the two pieces together. Cut one side down from the top halfway. Cut the other side up from the bottom halfway.

Now slide the side cut from the bottom — down onto the top slit on the other side, hooking the two sides together.

Sometimes it works best to cut the slits at a slight angle as shown.

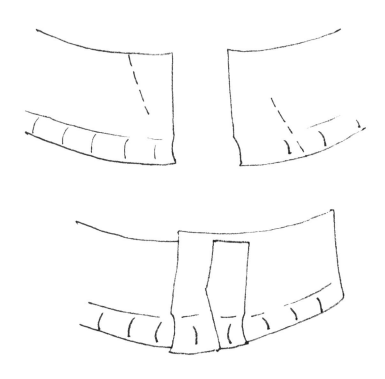

TEACHING THEMES

BUSY BEES

For Two's and Three's
Day-by-day, hands-on projects and activities are just right for busy little ones.

Busy Bees–FALL
For fall fun and learning, these attention-getting activities include songs, rhymes, snacks, movements, art, and science projects. 136 pp.
WPH 2405

Busy Bees–WINTER
Enchant toddlers through winter with a wealth of seasonal ideas, from movement to art. 136 pp.
WPH 2406

Busy Bees–SPRING
More than 60 age-appropriate activities enhance learning for busy minds and bodies. 136 pp.
WPH 2407

Busy Bees–SUMMER
Encourage toddlers to build, develop, and explore with their senses and turn summer fun into learning. 136 pp.
WPH 2408

CELEBRATIONS

Expand on your children's love for celebrations with these ideas for special learning fun.

Small World Celebrations
Multicultural Units • 160 pp.
WPH 0701

Special Day Celebrations
Nontraditional Units • 128 pp.
WPH 0702

Yankee Doodle Birthday Celebrations
Antibias Units • 128 pp.
WPH 0703

Great Big Holiday Celebrations
Traditional Units • 228 pp.
WPH 0704

PLAY & LEARN

This creative, hands-on series explores the versatile play and learn opportunities of a familiar object. Perfect for working with young children ages 3 to 8. Each 64 pp.

Play & Learn with Photos
WPH 2303

Play & Learn with Magnets
WPH 2301

Play & Learn with Rubber Stamps
WPH 2302

THEME-A-SAURUS

Capture special teaching moments with instant theme ideas that cover around-the-curriculum activities.

Theme-A-Saurus
50 teaching themes—from Apples to Zebras—plus 600 fun and educational activity ideas. 280 pp.
WPH 1001

Theme-A-Saurus II
Sixty more teaching units—from Ants to Zippers—for hands-on learning experiences. 280 pp.
WPH 1002

Toddler Theme-A-Saurus
Sixty teaching themes combine safe, appropriate materials with creative activity ideas. 280 pp.
WPH 1003

Alphabet Theme-A-Saurus
From A to Z—26 giant letter recognition units filled with hands-on activities introduce young children to the *ABC's*. 280 pp.
WPH 1004

Nursery Rhyme Theme-A-Saurus
Capture the interest children have for nursery rhymes and extend it into learning. 160 pp.
WPH 1005

Storytime Theme-A-Saurus
Flannelboard patterns accompany 12 storytime favorites, plus hands-on activities and songs. 160 pp.
WPH 1006

EXPLORING SERIES

Environments
Selected environments become very real places in this book series that encourages exploration. Hands-on activities emphasize all the curriculum areas. Each book begins with the "known" and lets the curriculum expand as far as children's interests can stretch.

Exploring Sand and the Desert
WPH 1801

Exploring Water and the Ocean
WPH 1802

Exploring Wood and the Forest
WPH 1803

TEACHER RESOURCES

1001 SERIES

These super reference books are filled with just the right solution, prop, or poem to get your projects going. Creative, inexpensive ideas await you!

1001 Teaching Props
The ultimate how-to prop book to plan projects and equip discovery centers. Comprehensive materials index lets you create projects with recyclable materials. 248 pp.
WPH 1501

1001 Teaching Tips
Shortcuts to success for busy teachers on limited budgets. Curriculum, room, and special times tips—even a subject index. 208 pp.
WPH 1502

1001 Rhymes & Fingerplays
A complete language resource for parents and teachers! Rhymes for all occasions, plus poems about self-esteem, families, special needs, and more. 312 pp.
WPH 1503

1•2•3 SERIES

These books present simple, hands-on activities that reflect Totline's commitment to providing open-ended, age-appropriate, cooperative, and no-lose experiences for working with preschool children.

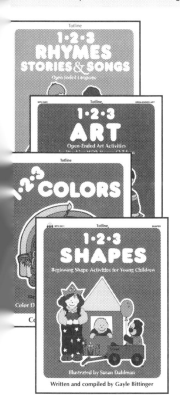

1•2•3 Art *Open-ended Art*
160 pages of art activities emphasize the creative process. All 238 activities use inexpensive, readily available materials. 160 pp.
WPH 0401

1•2•3 Colors
Hundreds of activities for Color Days, including art, learning games, language, science, movement, music, and snacks. 160 pp.
WPH 0403

1•2•3 Books
More than 20 simple concept books to make, including sequences, textures, and weather. 80 pp.
WPH 0406

1•2•3 Murals *Cooperative Art*
More than 50 simple murals to make from children's open-ended art. 80 pp.
WPH 0405

1•2•3 Reading & Writing
250 meaningful and non-threatening activities to develop pre-reading and pre-writing skills. 160 pp.
WPH 0407

BEAR HUGS SERIES

This unique series uses a positive approach for dealing with potential problem times. Great ideas for handling specific group situations. Each 24 pp.

Remembering the Rules
These simple rule reminders are fun and nonthreatening.
WPH 2501

Staying in Line
Make staying in line fun, quiet, and safe.
WPH 2502

Circle Time
Get children interested and involved in circle time.
WPH 2503

Transition Times
Help children smoothly shift focus from one activity to another.
WPH 2504

Time Out
Encourage reflective and therapeutic time outs that get results!
WPH 2505

Saying Goodbye
Ease separation anxiety with simple activities and gentle distractions.
WPH 2506

Nap Time
Guide reluctant children into quiet, restful moods.
WPH 2509

Meals and Snacks
Quiet young ones so they can eat without dampening their spirits.
WPH 2507

Cleanup
Encourage cooperation and speedy work with fun cleanup times.
WPH 2508

1•2•3 Rhymes, Stories & Songs *Open-ended Language*
Open-ended rhymes, stories, and songs for young children. 80 pp.
WPH 0408

NEW! 1•2•3 Shapes
Hundreds of activities for exploring the concept of shapes—circles, squares, triangles, rectangles, ovals, diamonds, hearts, and stars. 160 pp.
WPH 0411

1•2•3 Math
Hands-on activities, such as counting, sequencing, and sorting, help develop pre-math skills. 160 pp.
WPH 0409

1•2•3 Science
Develop science skills—observing, estimating, predicting—using ordinary household objects. 160 pp.
WPH 0410

1•2•3 Games *No-Lose Games*
Foster creativity and decision-making with 70 no-lose games for a variety of young ages. 80 pp.
WPH 0402

1•2•3 Puppets
More than 50 simple puppets to make to delight children. 80 pp.
WPH 0404

Instant Hands-on Ideas!

Totline® Newsletter and **Super Snack News** are perfect for working with young children because they are put together by the publisher of Totline® Books, a leader in early childhood resources for parents and teachers. Totline books and newsletters are guaranteed to be appropriate, enriching, and fun. Help your children feel good about themselves and their ability to learn by using the hands-on approach to active learning found in these two newsletters!

Warren Publishing House
P.O. Box 2250, Dept. Z, Everett, WA 98203

Totline Newsletter

This newsletter offers creative hands-on activities that are designed to be challenging for children ages 2 to 6, yet easy for teachers and parents to do. Minimal preparation time is needed to make maximum use of common, inexpensive materials. Each bimonthly issue includes • seasonal fun • learning games • open-ended art • music and movement • language activities • science fun • reproducible teaching aids • reproducible parent-flyer pages and • Good Earth (environmental awareness) activities. *Totline Newsletter* is perfect for use with an antibias curriculum or to emphasize antibias values in a home environment.

Super Snack News

This newsletter is designed to be reproduced!

With each subscription you are permitted to make up to 200 copies per issue! They make great handouts to parents. Inside this monthly, four-page newsletter are healthy recipes and nutrition tips, plus related songs and activities for young children. Also provided are category guidelines for the CACFP reimbursement program. Sharing *Super Snack News* is a wonderful way to help promote quality childcare.

To receive your FREE copy of either Totline Newsletter or Super Snack News, call 1-800-773-7240.